P9-CES-205

WHAT TIME IS IT, MR. CROCODILE?

Judy Sierra

ILLUSTRATED BY Doug Cushman

SCHOLASTIC INC.
New York Toronto London Auckland Sydney
Mexico City New Delhi Hong Kong Buenos Aires

No part of this publication may be reproduced, stored in a retrieval system, or transmitted in any form or by any means, electronic, mechanical, photocopying, recording, or otherwise, without written permission of the publisher. For information regarding permission, write to Harcourt, Inc., 6277 Sea Harbor Drive, Orlando, FL 32887-6777.

ISBN-13: 978-O-545-O3815-7
ISBN-1O: O-545-O3815-4

Text copyright © 2004 by Judy Sierra
Illustrations copyright © 2004 by Doug Cushman
All rights reserved. Published by Scholastic Inc., 557 Broadway, New York, NY 10012, by arrangement with Harcourt, Inc. SCHOLASTIC and associated logos are trademarks and/or registered trademarks of Scholastic Inc.

12 11 10 9 8 7 6 5 4 3 2 1   7 8 9 10 11/0

Printed in the U.S.A.   40

This edition first printing, September 2007

The illustrations in this book were done in acrylic on gessoed Arches watercolor paper with collage additions.
The display type was set in Victoria Casual.
The text type was set in Neue Neuland and Victoria Casual.
Designed by Lydia D'moch

For irrepressible Lily
—J. S.

For Jackie, my true inspiration in Paris
—D. C.

Down by Bristlecone Bay, where the wifflefish play,
Mr. Crocodile, Esquire, is planning his day.

THINGS TO DO TOMORROW

9:00	wake up
10:00	eat breakfast
11:00	swim
12:00	go to town
1:00	visit the library
2:00	shop for food
3:00	bath and snack
4:00	catch those pesky monkeys
5:00	cook those pesky monkeys
6:00	eat those pesky monkeys
7:00	read a story
8:00	sing a lullaby to me

"Time to wiggle my toes. Time to put on my clothes.
Time to brush every tooth till it sparkles and glows."

"What TIME is it, Mr. Crocodile?"

"Time to start off my day at the Stingray Café,
with a barnacle bagel and sea-slug soufflé."

"WHAT TIME IS IT,
Mr. Crocodile?"

"Time to plunge in the bay,
time to splash, time to play.
Time to practice my
crocodile water ballet."

"WHAT TIME IS IT, MR. CROCODILE?"

"Time to roll into town.
Time to twirl round and round.
Time to skate right side up,
or—YIKES!—upside down."

"WHAT TIME IS IT, MR. CROCODILE?"

"Time to take a quick look
for a recipe book.
HURRY UP! HURRY UP!
I've got monkeys to cook."

Bananas I Have Loved

A Monkey's Tail

Apes in the FoG

King Kong My Side

Cooking AA-Aw

Pineapples

Oranges

Hot Peppers

MR. CROCODILE?"

"Time to shop where it's smart, at the Crocodile Mart.
How did all these BANANAS get into my cart?!?"

"Time to soak, time to dream,
time to plot, time to scheme.
Time to guzzle Croc-Cola
and seaweed ice cream."

"WHAT TIME IS IT, MR. CROCODILE?"

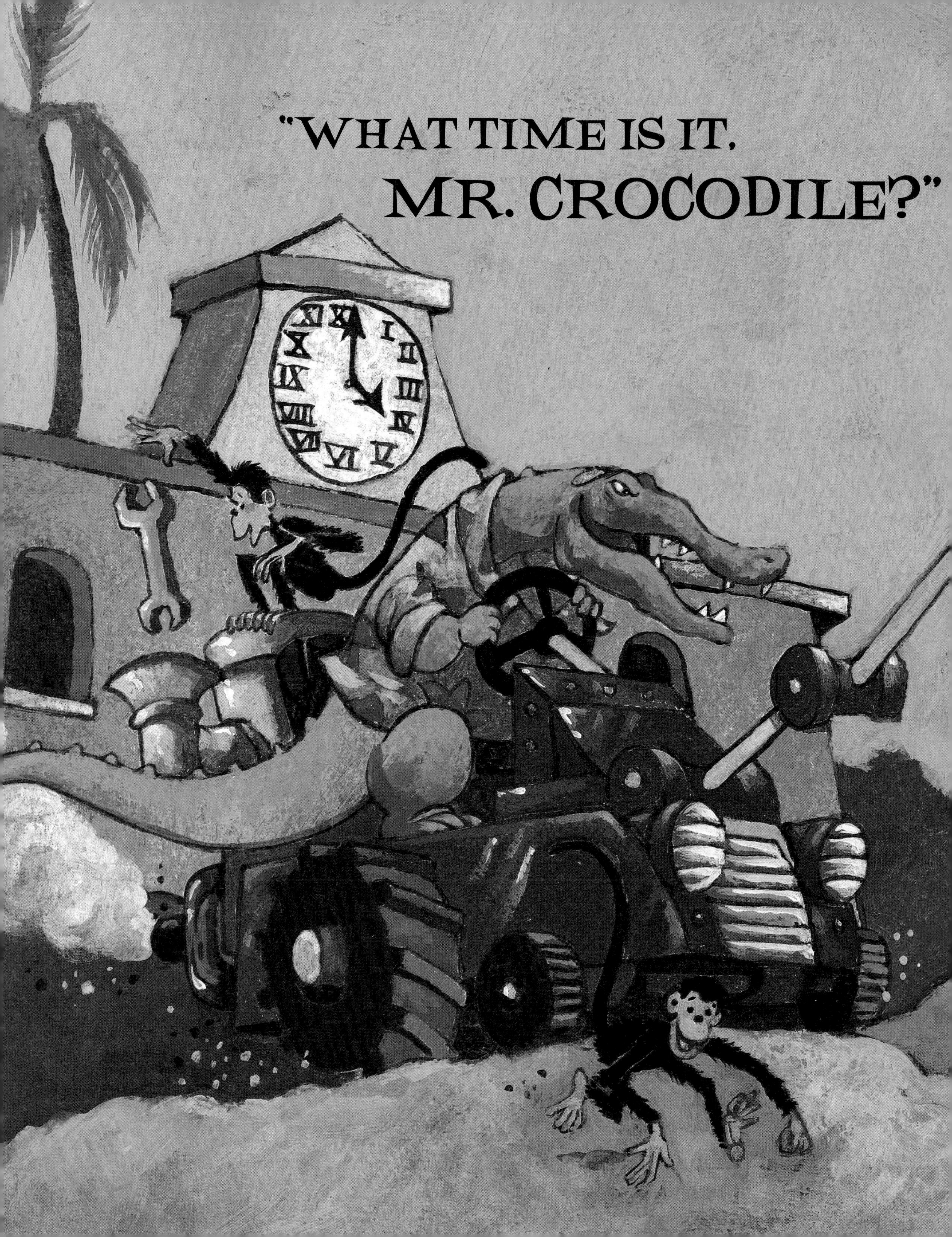

"Time to capture my meal as I sit at the wheel
of my marvelous monkey-collecting mobile."

"WHAT TIME IS IT, MR. CROCODILE?"

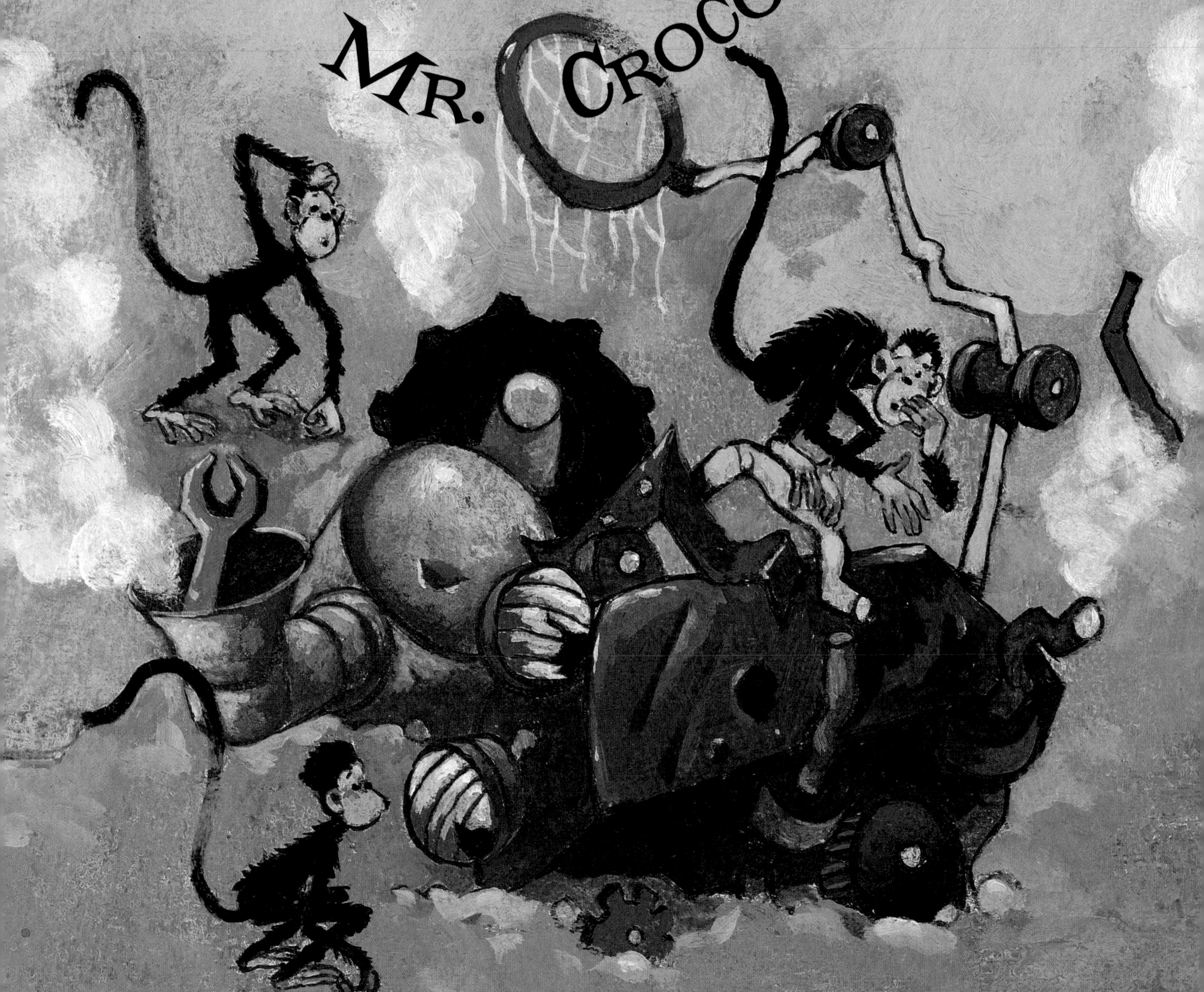

"Time to cook? I'm too tired. I am SO-O-O uninspired—
'cause my plan to catch monkeys completely backfired."

"Time to say, 'I was rude, with a bad attitude,
and I'd much rather have you as friends than as food.'"

"What time is it, Mr. Crocodile?"

"Time to read about Fred, who bumped his poor head, and the five little monkeys that bounced on his bed."

"What time is it,
Mr. Crocodile?"

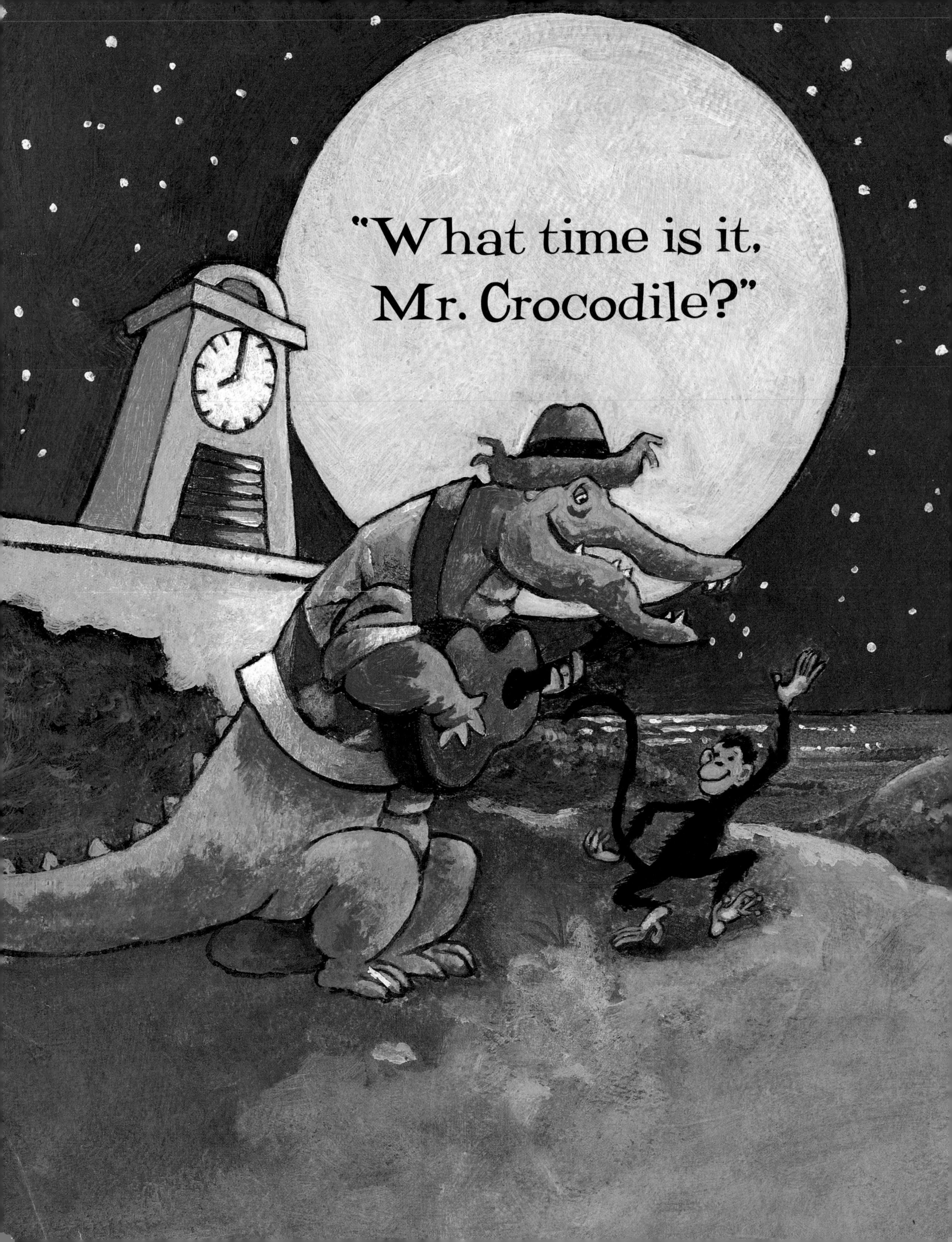

"Time to sing a sweet tune 'neath the crocodile moon.
Time to whisper, 'I hope you'll be coming back soon.'"

Down by Bristlecone Bay, where the wifflefish play,
Mr. Crocodile, Esquire, is planning his day.

THINGS TO DO TOMORROW

9:00   wake up

10:00   eat breakfast

11:00   teach monkeys to ∧ swim

12:00   go to town

1:00   visit the library — *get good monkey stories!*

2:00   shop for food — *lots of bananas!*

3:00   bath and snack

4:00   ∧ play catch ∧ with those ~~pesky~~ nice monkeys

5:00   cook ∧ for those ~~pesky~~ nice monkeys

6:00   eat ∧ with those ~~pesky~~ nice monkeys

7:00   read a story — *no bouncing this together time!*

8:00   sing a lullaby to ∧ ~~me~~